The
Storyteller's Secrets

The
Storyteller's
Secrets

Tony Mitton

Illustrated by
Peter Bailey

David Fickling Books

OXFORD · NEW YORK

A DAVID FICKLING BOOK

Visit us on the Web! www.randomhouse.com/kids

Educators and librarians, for a variety of teaching tools,
visit us at www.randomhouse.com/teachers

Library of Congress Cataloging-in-Publication Data is available upon request.
ISBN 978-0-385-75190-2 (trade) — ISBN 978-0-385-75191-9 (lib. bdg.)

MANUFACTURED IN CHINA
May 2010
10 9 8 7 6 5 4 3 2 1

First American Edition

*To anyone who ever told a story
and anyone who ever listened.*

T.M.

*For Osian and Inigo,
with love.*

P.B.

Not so very far from here, nor so very long from now, there were two children. Their names were Toby and Tess and they were twins. They lived with their mother in a cosy cottage beside a village green. In the middle of the green stood a great old chestnut tree, and beneath the tree was a stout wooden bench where Toby and Tess sat when they hadn't much to do or when there were things they wanted to talk about.

One day their mother shooed them out of the house. 'Go out,' she said. 'Go and play like children should. I've things to do and I can't be having you under my feet all day. The village is safe, the weather is good. And the fresh air will help you grow healthy and strong. I've made you a picnic for your lunch. Go out now and enjoy this fine day that the world has given you.'

Toby and Tess sat on the bench beneath the chestnut tree, wondering what the day would bring them, wondering where they should go and what they should do. And it was just at that moment that they first saw Teller.

Toby saw him first and nudged Tess. 'Look.'

'A stranger!' gasped Tess.

At a distance, against the skyline, all they could make out was a rather ragged silhouette. The figure was dressed in an old-fashioned robe, like a character in a story book. He held a staff in his right hand and on his back there was a bundle.

The stranger paused on the crest of the hill. He looked back the way he had come. Then he gazed all around him, as if surveying the world as far as he could see. Then he peered down into the village and began to take the path that led towards where Toby and Tess sat beneath the great old chestnut tree.

'He's coming this way!' said Toby.

As the stranger drew closer the children could see more and more of him. He was an old man with a weathered face, browned by the sun. His long, tousled hair was greying, as was his straggly beard. On his feet he wore stout leather sandals and in his hand his staff was like a knotty tree branch. Although he was old, he seemed sturdy, as if he could walk for miles if need be. And his eyes! How they twinkled with an air of mischief and mystery.

He was making for the bench as if he meant to sit down. So Toby and Tess got up, partly out of respect for a grown-up, and partly out of uneasiness about such an odd character.

He flumped down onto the bench and gave a grateful sigh.

'Ah,' he said wearily, 'how good to sit down at last.' He took a swig from a flask that was slung round his neck on a leather strap. 'Water. The stuff of life, eh? But no lunch for me today. The squirrels took it out of my bundle while I was resting. Cheeky little devils. Still, they have to live, I suppose. So they take what they can get. And today they got my lunch.'

'You can share our picnic,' said Toby. 'Our mother has sent us out of the house today. She's busy. I hate it when she makes us go out. I wanted to play indoors. But she's made us a picnic, so you can have some

of that if you like. It's cheese sandwiches, plums and home-made biscuits. She makes good biscuits.'

The old man smiled at Toby. 'What a very kind offer,' he said warmly. 'I should like that. But if I'm to share your lunch, I must give you something in return. Let me tell you a tale, an old story, a story about a mother who did not love, but hated instead, and about what happened as a result. Now I can see from this fine picnic of yours that you have a mother who loves you, who cares for you. And if she's turned you out of the house today, it's because she wants to clean and cook and make good so it's all the more welcoming for you when you go back to it this evening for your tea. But imagine a mother who wanted to cast you out for good and all, who wanted never to see you again and who hoped that you might perish in the woods so she need never be troubled by you anymore. Now, is that not a terrible thought?'

The children nodded. It was a terrible thought indeed.

'But I'm getting ahead of myself,' said the old man. 'If I'm to share your lunch and tell you one of my tales, I must introduce myself. And I should find out who I'm talking to as well. That is only good and proper.' He looked from one child to the other and said quite simply, 'My name is Teller. I am called that because I tell

The two children seated themselves on the soft grass and Teller began.

tales. Good ones. Old ones. From long ago. And you are . . . ?' he asked.

'Toby and Tess,' said Toby.

'All beginning with T,' said Teller. 'A trio of Ts. How curious. How tidy.' He settled himself more comfortably on the bench. 'Sit down, then,' he said, 'and I'll tell. I'll tell you this tale, and then we'll have that lunch.'

The two children seated themselves on the soft grass in front of the bench and Teller began.

The Woodcutter's Daughter

There once was a woodcutter lived in a wood.
His young daughter, Mary, was gentle and good.
But the little girl's mother was buried and dead,
and a stepmother stood in her place now instead.

The stepmother came with a child of her own,
whose heart, like her mother's, was cold as the stone.
When the woodcutter took up his axe and went out,
the mother and daughter would grumble and shout,

'Oh, Mary, come quickly, and clean up the sink.
Now stitch up my stockings and fetch me a drink.
Then clean out the fireplace and sweep up the floor,
and wash all the windows and polish the door.'

They'd boss and they'd bully. They'd rant and they'd moan.
And Mary felt miserable, sad and alone.
But Mary grew pretty and graceful and tall,
and the woodcutter loved her the best of them all.

Now this made the others hate Mary the worse,
so the stepmother gritted her teeth in a curse:
'I'll set her a task in the depths of the wood,
a task that will rid us of Mary for good!'

It was deep in the winter, with snow all around,
and everything frozen, yes, even the ground.
The stepmother led Mary out to the gate,
then she uttered these words in a mouthful of hate:

'Gather me strawberries, juicy red strawberries,
out in the wilderness, deep in the snow.
Never come back till you've gathered such strawberries.
Pick up your basket and go!'

Poor Mary went quietly, off on her way.
She could not resist, so she had to obey.
She knew that no berries could grow in that cold,
but her stepmother's hate made her do as was told.

She walked through the wilderness, chilly and white,
as the day drained away to the darkness of night.
She thought that her life would be lost in that dark
when suddenly Hope lighted up like a spark!

For there, through the trees, she saw orange and gold.
'A fire,' she murmured, 'to keep out the cold.'
There were folk round the fire, all warming themselves,
and to Mary's surprise, it was twelve little elves!

'Now, Mary,' said one, 'don't be shy, never fear.
Our fire will warm you. Be bold and draw near.
We're the elves of the months, and we know who you are.
If it's berries you seek, then you need not go far.

'My brother July will soon fill up your basket . . .
You see – it is done! You had barely to ask it.
Your basket is brimful of strawberries red.
Now my brother will lead you straight back to your bed.'

July chose a fire-coal, glowing and bright,
then he led Mary back through the depths of the night.
And when they returned, though her stepmother smiled,
her eyes seemed to glitter so bitter and wild.

So the next time the woodcutter went on his way,
Mary's stepmother called her to smile and to say,
'Go out through the snow, Mary. Take a long ramble.
And find us some blackberries, ripe on the bramble:

'Gather me blackberries, purple, plump blackberries,
out in the wilderness, far in the snow.
Never come back till you've gathered such blackberries.
Pick up your basket and go!'

Well, Mary went quickly, for this time she knew
just where she could go, and indeed what to do.
For she knew that the elves would assist in her task.
She had only to go to their fire and ask.

She walked till she spied the bright glow of the fire,
and this time the flames seemed to crackle yet higher.
Then up got the leader with, 'Mary, my dear,
you've come for your blackberries. Look. They are here.'

October said, 'Truly. Believe it, my child.'
And Mary's big basket was instantly piled.
The blackberries glistened, so plump and so fine,
and the juice trickled out of them darkly as wine.

October then picked out a coal, big and bright,
and led Mary home by the glow of its light.
But when Mary's stepmother saw her return,
the hate in her heart made her bristle and burn.

'Now tell me your secret, for fruit will not grow
in the wintery wastes of the ice and the snow.'
So Mary then spoke of the twelve little elves,
who sat round their fire, all warming themselves.

'You foolish young wastrel! Those twelve little men
are told of in stories again and again.
You could have had rubies as red as ripe cherries!
You could have brought jewels. And yet you've brought berries.

'Now show us the way, and my daughter and I
will seek out the place where that fire leaps high.
We'll wish from those elf-men a pile of treasure,
and then we'll return to a life full of pleasure.'

So Mary then pointed, and watched them both go,
like little black beetles across the white snow.
And away they both went to that fire so bright,
where the flames seemed to whip at the edge of the night.

The leader approached from the rim of the fire.
'Now, what is your wish?' he began to enquire.
'We wish to have silver. We wish to have gold.
As much as our baskets can possibly hold.'

The leader could hear the greed in her voice.
'And so,' he commanded, 'you shall have your choice.'
He called out to March and said, 'Take them to where
the gold of the sunset bleeds over the air.

'And then take them up to the dark, hollow night,
where the needle-like stars prick their silvery light.
There's an endless supply of both silver and gold,
much more than their baskets can possibly hold.'

So March raised his wind and it whirled them away
to gather the gold from the end of the day,
then up to the darkness, so high and so far,
to sift out the silver from star upon star.

So March raised his wind and it whirled them away.

But whether they ever completed their task,
they never came back, so it's fruitless to ask.
Perhaps they still grasp at the glittering air,
with the cold in their hearts and the wind in their hair.

While the humble old woodcutter, here in the wood,
with Mary, his daughter, so gentle and good,
live simply and happily, ever and after,
warming their cottage with love and with laughter.

And what of the blaze with the twelve little men?
They're out in the forest till needed again.

'I'm so glad it all worked out for Mary in the end,' said Tess.

'And that she got to be happy in her nice, cosy cottage, too,' added Toby.

'Ah, yes, we all need a home to go back to,' said Teller. 'Even an old wanderer like me. Is that your home over there?' he asked, pointing.

'Why, yes,' said Tess.

'How did you guess?' asked Toby.

'Oh, just a hunch,' said Teller. 'It looks well looked after and loved and lived in. The kind of cottage where a good mother makes a picnic like this,' he said, looking down at the basket that held their lunch.

And as the three of them shared the food, Toby and Tess pointed out some of the other cottages that stood around the green. They told Teller who lived there and what they did and what they were like. The blacksmith, the carpenter, the weaver and so forth.

'I must be on my way soon,' said Teller as they finished the last of the biscuits. 'But let me leave you with one more short tale.

We've talked of homes, and this tale is about someone who needed a home for herself and her people. And how it required a bit of a miracle to get that home sorted out and settled. Will you hear it?'

'Oh, yes please,' said Tess.

St Brigid's Cloak

St Brigid, she went to the court
of the king
and she knelt on her bended knee.
'Please grant me,' she said,
'but an acre of land
for Our Lord and my sisters and me.'

But the king he was stubborn,
the king he was stern,
there was stone in his heart and his eye.
'You can have as much land,'
he said to the saint,
'as you and your sisters can buy.'

For she and her sisters,
the king well knew,
lived light in the lap of the Lord.
'You can have as much land,'
he cunningly crooned,
'as the pence in your purse
can afford.'

'The way for the rich into heaven,' said the saint,
'may show, if you succour the poor.
If you give but a little, a token at least,
it may serve you to loosen the door.'

St Brigid fell silent and stared at the ground,
then these were the words that she spoke:
'Could you find in your heart to willingly part
with such land as I drape with my cloak?'

The king gave a gesture of sudden impatience.
'Now, sister,' he cried, 'let it be!
The land you can clothe in your tattered old cloak,
such land you may have without fee.

'But when you have claimed it, begone from my sight
and never come asking me more.
The land you can see, it belongs but to me,
for the land is the king's, by God's Law.'

St Brigid said nothing, but loosened her cloak,
which four sisters came forward to hold.
They made as to spread it upon the small ground,
when a miracle seemed to unfold.

For, as at the corners they started to pull,
the cloak seemed to stretch and to spread.
The faster they tautened, the faster it grew,
till across the broad meadows they sped.

The four sisters rose on the wings of the wind
and it blew them across the wide land,
till all of the lea, from the hills to the sea,
was by Brigid's broad mantle full spanned.

The four sisters rose on the wings of the wind.

'Enough!' cried the king.
'You have shamed me today
with the play of your miracle cloak.
You have taken my land from the
hills to the strand.
You have stripped me of all
at a stroke.'

But Brigid said, 'Only so much
do we ask as to harbour our house
and our living.
The land lies before you and
you are the king.
The gift is still yours for the giving.'

So the king gave them gratefully
all that they asked.
He marked out the plot with his sword.
Then he cried, 'All who stand
in the bounds of this land
are under the cape of the Lord.'

And Brigid said, 'Any who come to this place
after this blessing today,
whether they come bringing hunger or grief,
shall never go empty away.'

As the last words died on the air, the three of them sat silent, their heads still full of the story that had just been. Then Teller reached into the bundle that lay at his feet on the grass. From it he took a leather pouch tied up with a leather lace. He untied the lace, reached inside, felt about for a moment, then took out two small scraps of something.

'Put out your hands,' he said to the children.

Bemused, they did as he asked. Into each of their right hands he put one of the objects. At first it was not clear what they were. The children both squinted, first at their own hand and then at the hand of the other.

'Mine looks like some kind of dried-up, shrivelled berry,' said Tess, mystified.

'And mine's a scrap of cloth, I think,' said Toby.

Teller pointed to each hand in turn as he spoke. 'The berry is

one of the berries that the woodcutter's daughter brought back from the forest,' he said. 'And that scrap of cloth is a fragment of St Brigid's cloak. The very same,' he added with emphasis.

'But where did you get them?' pressed Toby.

'Yes,' said Tess. 'And how can you be sure?'

'Handed on,' said Teller. 'On and down. Like I'm doing again now.'

'But what shall we do with them?' asked Tess.

'Keep them,' replied Teller. 'Just keep them. On your windowsill. In a bowl. Somewhere you can see them often. To remind you and keep the story fresh in your memory. Think of them as curios, as curiosities. Things that can't be measured with money, or bought or sold. But things of special value, with magical force. Story power, you could say. I may have more for you when I call again, to add to your collection.'

'Will you call again?' said Toby.

'Yes, when?' added Tess. Both children were fascinated by this strange old man and his odd stories, and they were now reluctant to see him go.

'When I can,' said Teller. 'When I can. But in the meantime you have those two small treasures to remind you of the tales I've told.'

At the mention of 'treasures,' Toby and Tess both looked down into their palms at the little objects that Teller had given them. When they looked up again, Teller had gone and there was no other sign of him having been there.

* * *

The two children were walking out onto the green. Tess was carrying a small wicker cage and Toby was peering into it anxiously. They had been looking after an injured bird now for a couple of weeks and they thought it might be time to release it back into the wild.

'It's time,' their mother had said. 'If it's not strong enough now, it never will be. You can't go on keeping it indoors, shut up in that cage like a pet. The way it's fluttering makes me feel it's ready to fly again.'

'I hope its wing is properly mended,' said Toby as they arrived at the middle of the green.

'We'll soon see,' said Tess. And she reached in gingerly and tried to cup it in her hands.

'Here, let me,' said a voice behind them.

Toby and Tess both turned their heads

in surprise. 'Teller!' they exclaimed.

'How did you get here?' asked Toby.

But Teller ignored the question and looked into the cage. He reached in and with expert hands took hold of the bird. He drew it out and felt it gently all over, looking away thoughtfully as he did so.

'It'll be fine now,' he said confidently. He glanced sideways at the children and said, 'Wish it well as I give it back to the air.'

'Oh, goodbye, little bird,' said Tess.

'Yes, goodbye,' said Toby. 'Fly away free.'

Teller threw his hands into the air, opening them as he did so. For a moment the bird fluttered frantically just above their heads. Then a gust of wind caught it and it was borne aloft to soar into the distance. Soon it was no more than a tiny speck in the sky.

'You did well there,' said Teller. 'You saved a little life. That was an act of kindness. The world is a better place for every small act like that.'

'What else could we have done?' said Toby.

'Yes,' said Tess. 'The poor bird was injured. It needed our help.'

'You would be surprised what cruelty and what carelessness

It was borne aloft to soar into the distance.

people can be capable of, especially out there in the wide world beyond your village,' said Teller with a note of sadness in his voice. 'Let me tell you a tale about that. We are just a few steps from our story seat,' he added, nodding towards the chestnut tree and the bench beneath.

The Seal Hunter

Here is a story handed down
from many a year ago.
The tale's been told by many a tongue,
but I shall tell it so.

Duncan MacKinnon was a fisherman.
He sold his catch for a fee.
He lived in a lonely stone-built croft
by the side of the ragged sea.

And when he could, he would hunt the seals
and strip them of their hides.
He would keep and cure each precious pelt
but throw each corpse to the tides.

Now in those days the pelts were prized
and folk would pay full well
for a sealskin cap, or a bag, or boots,
or clothes, as I've heard tell.

And the local folk came knocking
at the sealskin seller's door,
so in time he left his floats and nets
and hunted seals the more.

Duncan MacKinnon rowed the tides.
At his belt he wore a knife.
And with the aid of its deadly blade
he would take each sad seal's life.

The hunter soon grew stout and rich
with the sale of the skins he caught.
He lived his life by the skill of his knife,
but gave the seals small thought.

It was on a day, in a sunlit bay,
when the whole sea seemed to smile,
he sighted a huge and handsome seal
stretched out on a rocky isle.

When he saw the size of the great grey seal,
he crooned, 'With a skin like that
you could trim and shape a costly cape
or many a shoe and hat.'

Duncan MacKinnon rowed the tides.

So he moored his boat but a short way off
and he crept up, yard by yard.
Then, almost there, he leaped through the air
and he drove his knife in hard.

But the great grey seal was a fighter,
and he writhed from the hunter's grip.
With the knife in his side he dived for the tide
and he gave his man the slip.

MacKinnon shrugged and returned to his boat
to row to his own home shore.
'The seals in the sea swim wide and free,'
he mused. 'There are plenty more.'

Duncan MacKinnon, oh, Duncan MacKinnon,
now take great heed, beware.
The fill of a purse can be a curse
for living things to bear.

The clink of a coin and its comfort
may keep you warm and dry.
But what of the shame that sticks to your name
at each sad creature's cry?

What is the worth of a wealth that's ripped
from the world by a ruthless knife?
What of the guilt on which it's built
as you strip each struggling life?

Duncan MacKinnon, when you were a boy,
did you never sit down on the beach
to learn from the pound of the stern sea-sound
the lessons that it might teach?

Faithless fisherman, when you were young,
did nobody think to tell
that there's more in the sea than a hunter's fee,
there's life in the great grey swell?

Did nobody show you, upon the shore,
when you were both young and small,
that the rolling sea, so fair and free,
is the Ancient Mother of All?

Sad seal hunter, learn in time,
as you stack your brimming store,
when simple need grows into greed,
there'll be darkness at your door.

Late that night, as he sat by the light
of his guttering oil-lamp flame,
there came a knock at his low croft door
and a voice called out his name.

In a place so lone, at an hour so late,
who could this caller be?
The curious hunter loosed the door
and peered out cautiously.

There on the threshold stood a man
in a cape both dark and long.
He spoke to the wary hunter
in a deep voice, soft yet strong:

'Duncan MacKinnon, say, is it so,
you have seal skins here to sell?
Are you that famous hunter
of whom the folk all tell?'

Duncan MacKinnon nodded.
'Of skins I have full store.
I'll sell you all the skins you need.
The sea holds plenty more.'

The dark-caped stranger listened
to the words the hunter told.
'My master waits nearby,' he said,
'if you wish your skins all sold.'

Duncan MacKinnon and the stranger
walked out to the edge of the land.
'Now where,' said the man, 'is my master?
He was here just now, at hand . . .'

They peered at the edge of the clifftop
where the brink might break and slip.
It was then that the hunter felt his arms
held tight in a vice-like grip.

And before he could make a murmur
or shake his pinned arms free,
the stranger leaped from the clifftop
and they plummeted down to the sea.

As they hit the cold and dark of the waves,
the stranger pulled him down.
The hunter felt his life was done,
for now he must surely drown.

Down they went, far deep beneath
the foam and the rolling waves,
till they came to an underwater world
where the rocks were pierced with caves.

Still he felt the stranger's hands
where they gripped his arms so tight,
as together they swam through the mouth of a cave
and into a greeny light.

And down in that weird and greeny light
where he thought to meet his death,
when his will gave way and he drank the brine,
he found he could draw his breath.

Now as he drank that liquid brine
he felt both light and free.
And the eerie glide of his sinister ride
seemed neither of land nor sea.

It was then that he noticed the skin of his guide
had a silky, a slippery feel.
In the watery light he saw to his fright
that the man had become a seal.

Gone were the hands and gone were the feet,
and gone was the long black cape.
For now the dark guide that he floated beside
was wholly a seal in shape.

His silent seal-guide drew him on
to an underwater town
where the walls shone white with a pearly light
and the seals swam up and down.

They swam till they came to a palace
and they passed on through its door.
And once inside his eyes went wide
at the sight the hunter saw.

There were white rock seats in a circle,
where many a seal sat round.
But in that solemn circus
there came not ever a sound.

For there in the circle's centre,
set out on a white rock bed,
lay a seal so still and silent
it seemed that seal lay dead.

Then the hunter saw the knife in its side
and he opened his mouth to moan.
There on its hilt was the ring of gilt
that marked it as his own.

He fell to his knees on the chamber floor
and wrung his hands in fear.
Alone, deep down in the selkie town,
he sensed his end was near.

But the seal-guide's voice spoke up to him
and seemed to fill his head.
'Remove the knife and smoothe the wound,'
that strange voice softly said.

The hunter pulled his cruel knife out
and wiped its blade of steel.
When, with his hand, he smoothed the wound,
he saw it swiftly heal.

The great seal stirred and seemed to stretch,
then reared up proud and high.
He turned toward the hunter
and fixed him with his eye.

'I am the king of the seals,' he said.
'Your seal-guide is my son.
The time has come to settle up
the deeds that you have done.

'Tonight my son has brought you here
to gather back your knife.
And if you now repent your deeds,
I'll grant you back your life.

'If you will fish the seas again
and do the seals no ill,
we seals will always be your friends
and help your nets to fill.

'But if you slay a seal once more
and take it for its skin,
the selkie folk will seek you out
and slay you for your sin.

'Now stand again, and sheathe your knife
and say before us now,
will you give up the hunter's life
and take The Selkie Vow?'

The hunter rose and sheathed his knife,
then, there upon the sand,
he saw appear these words so clear,
as if by secret hand:

I, who live by swell of sea,
will learn to use it modestly,
to fish it but for honest need,
and not to grasp with rising greed.

I, who ride on wealth of wave,
will vow to cherish, succour, save,
never to pluck or cruelly plunder
what goes over, on or under.

I, who tell the turning tide,
will make the sea my place, my pride,
and guard all things that go within,
whether of scale or shell or skin.

I, who live beside the shore,
will know content, not ask for more.
I am for her, and she for me.
The Selkie Vow respects the sea.

The hunter stood and took the vow,
and at each word he spoke,
the darkness seemed to gather round
and wrap him like a cloak.

He fell into a deep-sea swoon
where waters rolled him round.
And when he woke it seemed to him,
he lay on solid ground.

He raised his head and looked about.
The moon shone sweet and soft.
Above him on the cliff he saw
his stony fisher-croft.

He climbed the path and found his door,
then stumbled to his bed.
And all that night the strange events
went reeling through his head.

But when the light of early dawn
came trickling through his pane,
he rose to fetch his fishing nets
and cast them once again.

And, from that time, if traders,
skin dealers, came to call,
he'd show them where his dagger hung,
sheathed safely on the wall.

He'd sit them at his table
and tell his story through,
of how he met the selkie folk,
and the king he nearly slew.

And how again he fished the sea
and looked to it for life,
but never more would harm a seal
with net or club or knife.

And how, whenever he rode the waves,
in swollen tides or calm,
his nets were never empty
and he never came to harm.

My story's done and over,
my tale is at an end,
of how a cruel hunter
became the selkies' friend.

It is a story handed down
from many a year ago.
The tale's been told by many a tongue,
but I have told it so.

'Oh, what a strange story,' said Tess.

'Like being taken to another world,' said Toby.

'There's the power of story for you,' said Teller. 'It can take you places you might never get to in your body. And it can teach you things by telling tales that seem unbelievable . . .'

'How did you know about the bird?' asked Toby.

'And to be here just at the right time?' said Tess.

'Ah,' said Teller mysteriously, with a twinkle in his eyes. 'News gets around in all kinds of ways. But I have something for you in my bag. To go with the story, of course.' And he rummaged in his bundle, took out the leather pouch, and from it seemed to conjure another of his little scraps. It looked like a tangle of black, tarry string.

'What is it?' asked Tess.

'Yes, where's it from?' added Toby.

'It's a scrap of the seal hunter's fishing net,' answered Teller, putting it into Tess's hand. 'Add it to your collection. If you forget the story, just sniff the net. You can almost smell the sea on it. Maybe the seals too,' he said, wrinkling up his nose. 'I must be off now, though,' he went on briskly. 'Places to go, people to see. While I still have the strength,' he added.

And leaving Tess holding the piece of net, and both twins watching him go, Teller hoisted up his bundle and took the track up and over the hill, returning the way he'd come the first time they'd seen him. He paused on the skyline for a moment, gave a brief wave, then disappeared out of sight.

Tess had had such a vivid dream in the night. It was so clear in her head when she woke up that she had to tell Toby about it straight away.

'I dreamed that the two of us found an old map in a dusty cupboard and the map showed treasure buried in the roots of the chestnut tree. In the dream we took picks and shovels and went digging there. We found a trapdoor with stairs leading down from it. So we took a candle lantern with us and found a whole vault, a cavern full of sparkling, glistening treasure, like in a picture book, jewels and gold and crowns and silver coins. It was so real, Toby, I have to go and look under the chestnut tree.'

So out she went to see for herself, with Toby hurrying to keep up with her. As the two children approached the tree, they saw a familiar figure sitting on the bench beneath it. He smiled mysteriously at them as they called out.

'Teller!' said Toby.

'What are you doing here?' said Tess.

'Treasure!' replied Teller, and his eyes glittered like gems. 'I've come to tell you a tale about treasure. A little bird tells me you've been dreaming about treasure. So I have just the tale for you.'

'But how did you know?' said Tess. 'I've only told Toby.'

We took a candle lantern with us.

Teller continued, ignoring her. 'Now this story is about treasure and dreams and journeys.'

The children could tell there was no use pressing him and they knew now that a story from Teller was not to be missed. So they sat down on the grass as usual while Teller began.

The Pedlar of Swaffham

One morning in Swaffham
a pedlar awoke.
He gazed at the ceiling
and here's what he spoke:

'I dreamed in the night
that a voice in my mind
said, "Go off to London
your fortune to find."'

'Ah, dreams,' said his wife.
'Now if dreams could come true,
I might not be me
and you might not be you.

'But as you're a pedlar
and walking's your way,
there's nothing to stop you
from leaving today.

'Your bag's at the ready.
It's waiting downstairs.
So go off to London
and peddle your wares.'

So off went the pedlar,
his dog at his feet,
to peddle his wares
to the people he'd meet.

And the words of his wife
seemed to hang at his ear:
'To follow their dream
is what many folk fear.

'But if you've a dream,
you should go where it leads.
Something to seek
is what everyone needs.

'It may turn out true
or be empty and hollow,
but nothing's to gain
if you won't up and follow.'

The journey to London
was one he knew well.
He stopped now and then
for he'd items to sell.

The journey to London was one he knew well.

But in time he arrived
and he set out to see
the place where the dream
said his fortune would be.

It was old London Bridge
and, way back in those days,
the bridge was a wonderful,
curious maze

of buskers and hawkers
and all kinds of shop,
where bustle and business
seemed never to stop.

He took up a pitch
by a greengrocer's stall.
Then he sat and he waited
for Fortune to call.

Now, day followed day
and, strangely to tell,
not a soul came to see
what he laid out to sell.

But with dogged persistence
he stuck to his post,
for to fathom his dream
was what ruled him the most.

When the pedlar had waited there
almost a week,
the greengrocer hailed him
and started to speak:

'Forgive me for saying,
but it seems that your pitch
is hardly the way
to do well and get rich.

'If I were a pedlar,
I'd visit the fairs,
for that's where you're likely
to peddle your wares.'

'It's a dream that I'm after,'
our pedlar replied,
'but I'm darned if I know
how to catch it,' he sighed.

'A voice in a dream
told me, steady and clear,
that a fortune awaited me,
now, and right here . . .'

'Ah, dreams,' smiled the greengrocer.
'That's what you chase . . .'
And a quizzical look
seemed to shadow his face.

'Well, I've had a dream now,
for over a year,
of a small country cottage –
the vision's so clear!

'At the end of its garden
an old plum tree stands,
and, there in the dream,
I've a spade in my hands.

'And I know if I search
in its roots, underground,
a fabulous fortune
is there to be found.

'But where the place is,
well, I haven't a clue.
I've no way of guessing
such secrets, have you?'

The pedlar was packing
his bag with his gear.
'You're right,' he said, smiling.
'My time is done here.

'I'm grateful I came
and I'm glad that we met.
But my dream's moving on
and I'll follow it yet.'

The pedlar and greengrocer
said their goodbye,
and the pedlar went off
with a gleam in his eye.

* * *

His wife was just hanging
the clothes on the line
when the pedlar blew in
looking breezy and fine.

'I think I've found out
how a fortune is made,'
he said as he sped
to the shed for his spade.

'Just a minute,' his wife called,
'but, beggin' your pardon,
I hope you're not planning
to dig up our garden?'

'Just the plum at the bottom,'
the pedlar replied.
'But it's going to blossom!'
his wife sadly cried.

The pedlar was already digging away.

The pedlar was already
digging away
as his poor wife looked on
with a face of dismay.

It seemed that her husband
was out of his mind.
In the tree roots, well, what
could he possibly find?

But the spade gave a jar
and a bit of a knock,
as if it had hit
on a cluster of rock.

The pedlar looked closer,
then murmured, 'Not rocks.
It's an ancient and curious
kind of a box.'

That box it was brimful
with silver and gold.
'We'll be rich,' said the pedlar,
'until we grow old.'

As they were, and they soon
became mayoress and mayor,
well known to be generous,
honest and fair.

And the fortune was used
for the welfare of all.
And they built a fine church
with a tower so tall.

The church, it still stands.
You may visit it there.
And the treasure tree, too,
it is rumoured, but where?

Though if you should dream
it holds treasure for you,
why, go there and seek it.
What else should you do?

* * *

Allow me to mention,
right here at the end,
an event that occurred
for our greengrocer friend.

He was minding his business
and tending his stall
when a messenger turned up
on horseback to call.

The messenger nodded,
with nothing to say,
delivered a package
and went on his way.

Now, what did the greengrocer's
strange package hold?
A purse that was bulging
with silver and gold.

And, in it, a message
which quietly said
these words that the greengrocer,
murmuring, read:

The silver it glimmers.
The gold it does gleam.
This treasure's a gift
from the garden you dream.

Your dream you thought meaningless,
empty as air.
But the plum has borne fruit
in this treasure to share.

'Oh, yes!' said Toby, his eyes shining. 'If I had a dream like that, I'd be off tomorrow.'

'Well, perhaps,' said Teller. 'But maybe it would be better to wait till you're just a bit older. Before going off travelling, I mean. The world is a big place. Meanwhile you can dream of course. But for now,' he continued, 'let me give you this.' And he picked up his twisty old staff. There was a little twiggy bit sticking out from the side of it, about halfway up. Teller snapped it off and handed it to Toby. 'There,' he said. 'For your collection. Another little bit of magic. Worthless to the eye, but special and powerful.'

'But how?' said Tess, looking puzzled.

'This staff. . . ,' replied Teller with a faraway look. 'This staff,' he repeated, 'once belonged to the pedlar of Swaffham himself. It's the very staff he carried with him on that magical journey. When

he became rich with the treasure, he rested the staff up against the wall by his fireplace. And there it stayed till the day he died, like a reminder to him of his great good fortune and how he had earned it. And in due course the staff fell into my hands, and with me it has stayed through all my journeys. I like to think it's brought me luck as well, if not the same kind of fortune. So now you have a little bit of it and it may bring you some luck also. At the very least, it will help you to remember the story. Which is one of my favourites, I think,' he said thoughtfully. He paused, then spoke again: 'I must be going now. So let me leave you with a trick. Hold onto the twig, now, both of you, one end each. Then shut your eyes and count to five.'

Puzzled, but curious, the children did as he said. When they got to five, they opened their eyes to find him gone. But there on the ground where he'd been standing lay a pile of golden coins, gleaming and shining in the sunlight. So bright were the coins that the children had to cover their eyes from the dazzle. And when they opened them again, the coins had gone and in their place were simply some fallen leaves from the chestnut tree, as if they'd been blown together in a pile by a mischievous breeze.

Toby and Tess were tidying the garden of their cottage with their mother. She'd made a posy of white roses from the briar that climbed up the cottage wall.

'Take it,' she said, 'and place it on your father's grave. He loved this bush and the white flowers it gives so freely.'

The two children were crossing the green with the posy, when Toby, who was holding it, tripped and dropped it. The posy fell to the ground, where it came apart. It was spoiled.

'Oh,' said Tess in disappointment.

'Oh,' echoed Toby, feeling foolish.

'Never mind,' came a voice from behind them. They turned round, startled, to see Teller there, as if by magic. Before they could even say his name, he continued, 'I can soon mend that. One

moment . . .' He bent and gathered the scattered posy in his old, brown hands. Then, as he stood up, he seemed to flourish it swiftly in his fingers until there it was again, good as new, before their very eyes.

'Oh, Teller!' exclaimed Tess.

'Yes, how did you . . . ?' trailed Toby.

'Go and complete your task now,' said Teller kindly. 'Then, when you've done, meet me back at the bench and I'll tell you a tale that begins with white roses just like these.'

The two children went to place the flowers on their father's grave, and when they returned, they found Teller sitting on the bench in his usual way. As they sat down on the grass, he began.

Tam Lin

Janet lived at the great high hall
with her father and all his men.
He was the laird of Carterhaugh
and he ruled that peaceful glen.

But folk there said that the greenwood
lay under a faery spell,
where Tam Lin guarded the wild white rose
that grew by the faery well.

Though nobody knew who Tam Lin was,
there were rumours his power was strong.
The old folk warned the young ones
by singing this country song:

Do not go to the wild green wood
for the faery folk rule there.
And never pluck the wild white rose
that breathes the woodland air.

But Janet was young and bonny
with a heart that loved a thrill.
And Janet's blood ran thick and red,
so full of fiery will.

Janet entered the greenwood,
where the breeze blew wild and weird.
She went and plucked the wild white rose
and strange Tam Lin appeared.

He was young and tall and handsome,
well dressed in elven green,
as fine a man as Janet
had ever dreamed or seen.

'Now who is it who dares,' he said,
'to brave this faery place?'
But Janet stood undaunted
and stared him in the face.

'I am Janet of Carterhaugh.
My father owns this wood.
The forest paths are mine to roam.
Let that be understood.'

Tam Lin smiled and shook his head.
'The faery queen rules here.
But while the sun shines through the leaves,
you have no need to fear.

'Come now with me. I'll show to you
the beauties that I mind.
The wood holds many a secret
well hid from human kind.'

So Tam Lin showed her through the wood
and taught her all its ways,
its magic flowers, enchanted bowers,
its mystic faery maze.

And when that day they bade farewell
at the forest brink, by the burn,
Tam Lin took Janet by the hand
and asked if she might return.

'You've only to come to the faery well,
where none but you will dare.
Pluck one white rose from the faery bush,
and I'll be standing there.'

And this she did full many a time,
for she went whenever she could.
She was scarcely seen at the castle now,
for her days were passed in the wood.

News soon came to her father
of the way her days went by.
So he sent for her and she came to him
and he looked her in the eye.

'Your days as a girl are done,' he said,
'for now you are full and grown.
It's soon you must up and wed, my dear,
else live your life alone.'

When Janet heard these words, Tam Lin
came pictured in her mind.
But how could a human lass like her
wed one of the faery kind?

She up and went to the wood at once
to ask him, fair and square,
was he a spirit or was he a man,
was he of flesh or air?

And when she was once again in the wood,
in the glade of the faery well,
Tam Lin appeared and she pressed him then
for all that he might tell.

'Now are you of the faery folk,
or are you mortal man?
And will you live one thousand years
or but a normal span?'

As *Tam Lin heard, a shadow seemed*
to pass from his troubled brow.
'Since you have asked directly,
I am free to tell you now . . .

'I come, like you, from the human world,
but a spell has held me in.
Your question here has quelled that spell.
My tale can at last begin.'

So Tam Lin told his story
as she sat and listened there.
His strange words wove an eerie mood
upon the woodland air.

'My father is Earl of Roxburgh
and I am his only child.
But since I became enchanted
I have lived in the woodland wild.

'As I rode by, one carefree day,
beside the faery mound,
a serpent started up my horse
and I tumbled to the ground.

'The faery queen lay waiting there.
She took me in her power.
This woodland is my prison now,
where I guard the white rose flower.

'And often when the nights are dark,
I join the faery band.
We ride the reaches of the sky
above the sleeping land.

'My life it passes easily.
My mistress treats me well.
There's little pain or hardship
within the faery dell.

'But once upon each seventh year
my queen must pay a fee –
one captive human sent to Hell
and soon it shall be me.

'So now I fear the searing fire.
I long to leave this place.
And I would be a man once more
among the human race.

'But I must meet a maiden
whose heart is brave and true.
And, as you stand before me,
I feel it might be you.

'For a maiden may release me
if she take me to her heart.
So tell me now, fair Janet,
could you wish to play that part?'

Janet looked at young Tam Lin
as he stood so firm and fine.
'I'll play that part and I'll be yours
if it means that you'll be mine.'

So Tam Lin told to Janet
the things that she must do
to win him back from faeryland
and bring the business through.

'Tomorrow night is Halloween,
when the faery queen's about.
She'll ride this way at midnight
with all her faery rout.

'You'll see me there among them
on a shining silver horse.
It's then you must lay hold of me
and pull me down by force.

'If you can keep a hold on me,
the faery power is gone.
Do not let go, whatever shape
I happen to put on.

'They'll turn me to a serpent,
a wild cat and a bear.
I may become some monstrous beast,
all claws and teeth and hair.

'But when I turn to red-hot iron
that scalds like fire from Hell,
it's then that you should haul me
and hurl me down the well.

'If I survive to clamber out,
released from faery charms,
you're then to wrap me in your cloak
and hold me in your arms.

'No faery then from crag or glen,
from woodland, field or moors,
will wield the power to hold me back
for I'll be ever yours.

'But if you dare not do these things,
I bid you now farewell.
No longer hope to find me here
for I'll be bound in Hell.'

Then Janet found herself alone,
and, where Tam Lin had stood,
the white rose gently wavered
within that old green wood.

And Janet knew what she must do
to disenchant Tam Lin.
She'd need much strength and courage
to try this task and win.

She went back to her father's hall
to pass the time between.
But all her mind was firmly fixed
on midnight, Halloween.

* * *

Janet stood by the greenwood.
The moon had risen high.
As midnight fell, the faery band
came brightly riding by.

The faery queen rode out in front
upon a horse of gold.
Such beauty and such radiance
were never seen nor told.

And there behind rode young Tam Lin
upon his silver mount
and then the faery retinue –
too many heads to count.

Janet drew one hasty breath,
preparing for her course.
She leaped and grasped at fair Tam Lin
and pulled him from his horse.

At once the faery queen whirled round
with widened eyes, aghast.
In awe the faery throng drew up
and watched the things that passed.

Tam Lin became a serpent
that bared its poisoned fangs.
But Janet winced and braced herself
to feel its biting pangs.

But then he was a wild cat,
with furious tooth and claw.
Bold Janet turned her face away
yet held on all the more.

And then Tam Lin grew monstrous,
a growling, powerful bear.
She kept her arms around him
and gripped his ragged hair.

He then became a gruesome thing
that mortal never saw.
Now Janet knew she must hold on,
though it frightened her full sore.

But as she gripped the harder,
his fur began to glow.
And soon the heat grew so intense
she longed to let him go.

He turned into a rod of iron,
all red and blistering hot.
She yearned to roll away from it
but knew that she must not.

With grim determination
she dragged it to the well.
She felt it drop and heard it splash.
Exhausted, down she fell.

She lay and waited by the well.
Now, would they lose or win?
At last a shape came clambering out . . .
the naked, gaunt Tam Lin.

She took her cloak of emerald green
and wrapped him tight around.
At that, the moonlit glade was filled
with tinkling, silvery sound.

The glade became a radiance
as bright as summer's day.
Then, as it dulled, the faery folk
had faded clean away.

Till nothing sinister was seen
around them in the wood,
and roses nodded quietly
beside them where they stood.

And this is where my story ends,
of Janet and her man,
where strange enchantments faded
and normal life began.

The mourning earl regained his son.
The laird of Carterhaugh
soon saw his daughter wedded
and the children that she bore.

And faery things seemed far away
and all dissolved and gone.
And the magic mound was plain, green ground
which children played upon.

'Just like those little ones over there,' said Teller, coming out of his story and back into the world of here and now. He pointed to a group of small children. 'Look at them playing there on the green grass, the way children have played since the world was young.'

'We used to play like that,' said Toby, smiling.

'And our knees were always dirty,' grinned Tess.

'But you're older now,' said Teller. 'And so am I. Time passes and we learn and grow. And my time is nearly up. So I've something to give you. First, a little token to go with the story, just like before.' He pulled the pouch from his bundle and rummaged around in it. Then he produced a small white dried flower.

'It's one of the rose heads from the bush where Janet picked that first white rose in the greenwoods, which made Tam Lin appear. Put it with your other treasures as a story speller. Though I doubt you'll need a speller for that story, since you have such a fine white rose bush climbing around your cottage door.'

Teller paused for a moment and looked around. 'This is a fine place you have here, a good village to grow up in. The cottages, the green, the whole feel of it all. It's a good place to begin and it would be a good place to end. But I've a feeling you'll be wanting to see a bit of the world in between. Some folk get restless, especially when they're young, and they need to see the world and to know what else is out there. And then some settle down, while others just go on wandering.'

'Is that what you do?' asked Tess.

'Yes, do you just go on wandering?' said Toby.

'Well, I have had a place to call home, a place to come back to now and then when I've wearied of my travels. But mostly I've spent my time wandering. On the go. And I've seen a fair few things, I can tell you. And heard even more. But, as I said, my time is up now so I have something special to hand on to you before I go. Listen for a moment. Just look and listen.'

Teller reached into his bundle and then, with a flourish, pulled something out and held it up in the air above his head. It was an ancient scroll made of parchment. He undid the cord which kept it

fastened and stood up in a serious, ceremonial way.

As he unrolled the scroll, Teller seemed to change strangely. He grew younger, straighter, taller and more impressive. There was a radiance around him, a kind of glamour, as if his very clothes were shining, as if his hair and beard were fuller and more vigorous. And when he spoke, his voice had a dignity they had not quite heard in it before.

He held the open scroll before their entranced eyes, and, as he spoke, the images on it shifted and shimmered as he mentioned each one. This was a map. A magical map. A Map of Marvels.

The Map of Marvels

My name is Merlin.
Of all magicians, once
I wore the crown.
But now I am old.
My fire is cold.
And my tower is tumbling down.
Here, in my hand, is my Map of Marvels.
But now my power is almost gone.
Now, my friends, as you stand before me,
the time has come to hand it on.

Keep it with you always.
Study it. Guard it well.
What it will bring as the years unroll,
no one can surely tell.
But mark, as I show you,
some of the marvels it portrays.
For these are among the strangest things
under the sun's rays.

Yes, here is the Map of Marvels,
torn at the edges, scorched, and tightly scrolled,
cracked with use, yellowed and ancient,
more precious than purest gold.
It was written and drawn in magical inks
on a fragment of dragon's hide.
See how the pictured ships seem to travel its waves,
and the painted rivers glisten and glide.

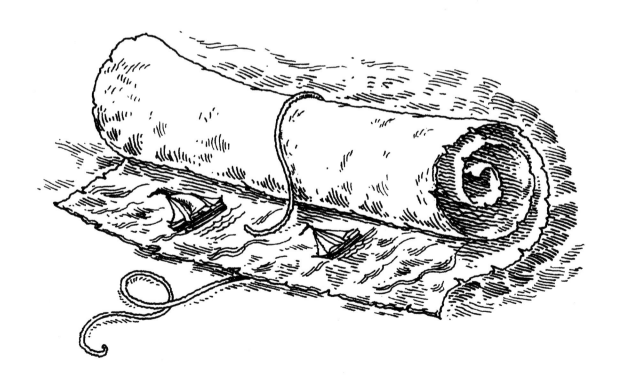

Look, down here is the Azure Sea,
where the gentle mer-folk sport and sing.
And here, to the north, deep in the pines,
is the Hall of the Mountain King.
And here is the Desert of Araby,
where the magic carpets fly.
And here, by my finger, the Cyclops' isle,
home of the giant with the single eye.

Here, to the west, are the Isles of the Blest,
where the magic apples shine in the sun.
See how a giant sleeps by the tree
to guard the fruits from all but One.
And here is the Whispering Forest,
where once I witnessed the phoenix rise and flap,
and a griffin coughed in the scarlet smoke,
and late in a glade by moonlight
a unicorn laid its horn in a maiden's lap.

But now I am old, and I ramble,
and I know that my time has almost come.
Of all the wonders I ever witnessed,
this Map of Marvels shows the sum.
So take it, make it your own,
for your faces tell you have travels in store.
Carry it with you on your journeys,
read its marvels, and yes . . . add more.

Notice this simple spot near the foot of the scroll.
It marks the mouth of a cave to a world below,
a shadowland of thought and dream and memory,
a place where only the dead may go.
To find my way there now, I need no map.
Take it. My route is simple. It is a way I know.

With these last words Teller let go of the map and it fluttered gently down to land on the ground in front of the two children, next to where the little white flower-head lay on the grass. It rested there, glistening magically for a moment, so that it captured their full attention. When they looked up again, Teller had gone. For a long while Toby and Tess just sat, full of silent wonder. And there on the grass in front of them lay a small, dry white rose and a curious old scroll, a Map of Marvels.

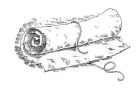

Five Fragments

a shrivelled old berry
that came from a wood
where a woodcutter's cottage
once quietly stood . . .

a fragment of cloth
from the edge of a cloak
once worn by a woman –
such wisdom she spoke . . .

a tangle of string
from an old tarry net
once used to catch fishes
all writhing and wet . . .

the tiniest twig
from a pedlar's stout staff –
he dug up some treasure,
then didn't he laugh . . . ?!

the head of a white rose
so withered and dry –

a sturdy lass plucked it
her fortune to try . . .

These are five fragments,
and each holds a spell:
a curious story
to cherish and tell.

They may look like rubbish,
so ragged and old,
but each has a value
more precious than gold.